MERRY & BRIGHT

A Summer Unplugged Novella

AMY SPARLING

Chapter One

Jett

My mom has really outdone herself this year. She's always been big on decorating for Christmas, (and every holiday, really) but this year my parent's house looks like it was made to be on the cover of a Christmas magazine. The porch has fake snow, tons of wreaths and garlands and clear lights all over the place. There are even wooden decor signs that say things like *Merry Christmas* and *Santa Stop Here*. It kind of looks like a Hobby Lobby set up shop on their front porch. And that's just the outside. I wonder what the inside looks like. Now that I've got a house of my own with my wife, I don't visit here as much as I used to, but that's also because I work at the family business next door, so I see my parents all the time, just not their house.

"Whoa," Keanna says as I turn into the driveway and park just in front of the garage. "Have they always had this many porch decorations?"

I laugh. "Definitely not. This is unfair. They're giving my sister a much cooler childhood than I got!"

My wife laughs and rolls her eyes. "Pah-leeze. You had a great childhood. I should know—I saw half of it."

I scoff, pretending to be offended. "Yeah right! You met me when I was a teenager. For all you know my childhood was sad and filled with zero fun decorations."

"Yeah right. I've seen every photo in your parents' house, and trust me, your childhood rocked."

There's no denying it. My parents are the best. And now that I've brought up this whole topic, I feel bad because Keanna's childhood sucked. She doesn't like to talk about it that much. She prefers to talk about all the things in her life that happened after she was adopted by my parent's best friends, Park and Becca. They also happened to live on the other side of the family business, so when they adopted her back when we were teens, she became my neighbor and my first (and only) love.

I lean across the front seat and kiss her cheek. "Why don't you go on inside and I'll bring in the presents?"

"You don't have to tell me twice," she says with a grin. "Being pregnant is awesome. I don't have to do anything anymore."

I grin, taking her enthusiasm as a sign that I'm being a good husband and soon-to-be-father. Our baby is due in a few weeks. I've read enough baby books to know that the next few months of new parenthood will be hard and full of sleepless nights, not just for Keanna but for both of us. Except I'm not the one growing a literal child in my body—she is. So I'm doing everything I can to make her life as easy and happy as possible.

I grab the presents from the back of my truck and head inside. My family consists of my parents, Keanna's parents, and us. We may not all be blood-related, but we're chosen family. To make holiday plans easy, we decided to alternate which house hosts Christmas, starting with this year at my parents' house. I'm not sure the rest of us will be able to top these decorations for when it's our turn to host. Mom must have had Dad working nonstop for days to get all of this put up.

The house smells like cinnamon and apple cider,

and a warm glow of holiday lights gives the atmosphere a real Christmasy vibe. I set all the presents under the massive tree in the living room and then find my wife and family in the kitchen. Mom has her hands on Keanna's belly while she gushes about how she can't wait to become a grandma. She and Keanna's mom, Becca, are still debating on what kind of grandparent name they want to be called.

"There he is," Dad says, clapping a hand on my shoulder. He's wearing a red and black buffalo plaid flannel shirt that matches Mom's. I resist the urge to make fun of him for twinning with Mom—and because if I mention it, Keanna might make me dress up in matching outfits with her one day.

"Damn, Dad—" I reach up and poke at his beard. He's never grown it out this long before but he was doing a "no shave November" thing last month and I guess he still hasn't felt like shaving. "Look at all this gray hair, old man!"

Dad scoffs. "It's just one or two gray hairs."

"It's a lot more than one or two," I say.

"I think it looks sexy," Mom says.

I make a barfing noise. My sister, Brooke laughs and makes the same sound.

You're never too old to make barfing noises when your parents do gross stuff like that.

Keanna's parents and little brother come over and we all gather in the living room with hot chocolate and appetizers, after a short debate on if we should open presents now or after dinner. Our little siblings want to open presents now. I voted for the food first, but I don't mind waiting. Keanna and I exchange or "real" gifts at home with each other. It's more special that way. But then we get each other fun gifts that we bring here to open in front of everyone. I'm ninety-nine percent sure she got me the new gaming console I want because she's really bad at being sneaky and she was asking me way too many questions about it over the last couple of weeks. I'm excited.

Dad tries to put motocross on the TV but mom tells him Christmas movies only. The moment my little sister hears the words "Christmas movies", she starts begging for Elf. I'm pretty sure she's watched it every single day this month and never gets tired of it.

With Elf playing on the TV, Dad and Keanna's dad, Park, start passing out presents, starting with the little kids who are the most excited. When he hands me a wrapped box, he says, "This one is for you and Keanna."

I told it out toward her. "You open it," she says, eyes wide with delight. "I already know what it is."

"How do you know what it is?" I ask, suddenly suspicious.

"Just open it!"

Keanna sits next to me while I tear off the paper. It's a white box you get from department stores, and they usually contain clothing. As I open it up and lift off the tissue paper, it's definitely clothing. Red and black buffalo plaid pajamas to be exact.

"We got two pairs," Keanna says. She's sitting cross-legged on the floor next to me, her hands resting on her stomach. "One for each of us! Isn't that awesome!"

I look around and realize that every single member of the family is all opening the same pair of matching pajamas while the women in the room smile mischievously at each other because they had planned this all along. At least it's just pajamas and I won't have to wear them out in public. Hopefully.

"Could be worse," Dad says, holding up his own set of red and black pajamas. "At least it's not a thong bathing suit!"

"Ooh, we should get the pool heater fixed," Mom says. "I forgot that it quit working a few weeks ago."

"Only if you promise I won't have to wear a Christmas thong," Dad says.

"I make no promises," Mom says in a hushed voice that I'm not sure I'm supposed to be able to hear.

"Ughhhhhhh," I say, rolling my eyes. "Gross."

"It would be so fun to have our own pool," Keanna says. "But I don't think our back yard is even big enough, so I'm glad we can come swim in yours."

"They're so expensive," Mom says. "Y'all are always welcome to use ours whenever you want. Don't get your own. Too much upkeep."

"They *are* expensive, but we basically stole ours," Dad says with a snort as he hands another present to my little sister.

"What do you mean?" I ask. "How do you steal a pool?"

"We didn't really steal a pool," Mom says. "It was kind of like we stole fifty grand, and then we used that money to get the pool installed in the backyard."

My jaw drops. "What?"

My parents exchange a look. Becca and Park chuckle to themselves.

"What's so funny?" I ask. "What on earth are you all talking about?"

"Technically, we legitimately earned the money," Dad says, holding up a finger. "It was just so easy, it kind of felt like we stole it. That was the easiest fifty grand I've ever earned."

"Ooh, this sounds interesting," Keanna says. She reaches for her mug of hot chocolate off the coffee table and cups it in both hands. "Do tell us how you earned this mysteriously easy fifty grand."

Mom takes a deep breath. "Well... it's been a while. I guess it was about twenty years ago? You were little," she says, nodding toward me.

"Jett was around five? Six?" Becca says. "We took care of him while you two were gone."

"Yeah, he was pretty small. I remember being sad about leaving him for a few days, but Jace convinced me that it would be fun to be on TV."

"Wait a minute... you were on TV?" I ask. I'm still dumbfounded that my parents have kept something like this from me for all these years.

"Not exactly," Dad says. "We were recruited for an episode of a reality TV show but they ever aired our episode."

"We still got paid though," Mom says.

"You were on REALITY TV?" I don't think my jaw can drop any further. "How did I not know about this?"

Both of my parents shrug. "I don't know. I guess it wasn't a big deal," Mom says. "They decided they couldn't put our episode on TV, so we just forgot about it."

"Why couldn't they put it on TV?" I ask.

"It wasn't dramatic enough," Dad says. "The producers threw everything they could think of at us to make it full of drama, but it didn't work."

"We love each other too much to let silly drama ruin our day," Mom says, looking at Dad. They share a loving smile.

"That is still so cool," Keanna says. "If so many of Jett's fans didn't absolutely hate me for being married to him, I'd think it would be fun to have our own TV show."

"We could call it The Track," Park says from across the room.

"That's what our business is called," Becca says, rolling her eyes.

"It would still make a good name for a TV show," he says, wrapping his arm around her.

"Please tell us more details," Keanna asks my parents. "I want to know absolutely everything."

"Me too," I say. There are a pile of presents next to me on the floor, but I don't care about them right now. This is more interesting. At least I think so—my sister and Keanna's little brother are still happily ripping open their own presents and squeeing at the contents.

"Well..." Mom's lips flatten as she ponders it. "I guess I could tell you the story."

"Every single detail," Keanna says.

"Okay," Mom says. She smiles warmly and tucks a strand of hair behind her ear. "Let's see...it was almost twenty years ago..."

Chapter Two

Bayleigh

Almost twenty years ago

I'M AT WORK, STANDING AT THE FRONT COUNTER AND staring at the computer, wondering if our business website for The Track really needs five different header images that splash across the page every few seconds, when the phone rings. My best friend Becca is usually here with me during regular business hours and she's the one who likes answering the phone, but she's having a dental cleaning right now so I'm the only one working this morning. Of course, I forget she's gone for a few seconds as the phone keeps ringing and ringing. Then I finally remember that Becca isn't here and I'm going to have to answer the phone.

I guess our weird header images problem can wait for a few minutes.

"Thank you for calling The Track! This is Bayleigh, how can I help you today?"

"Bayleigh Adams, you are just the person I'm looking for!" the voice on the other end of the phone says. It's a cheery, youthful, feminine voice. "My name is Angel Rivera. Actually," the voice says, I'm calling to talk to you *or* your husband—whichever one of you is the most adventurous!"

I snort out a laugh. "Well, he's the extreme sports motocross superstar, not me. I guess you could say he's more adventurous than I am, but he's out on the track giving lessons right now."

"That's fine, Mrs. Adams, I think you will be interested in what I have to offer you today."

"I'm listening..." My curiosity is piqued, that's for sure. People call us all the time but they always *want* something from us. Motocross lessons, interviews, photos, autographs. No one ever calls and offers us something.

"Mrs. Adams, I work with Xtreme TV Productions, and our viewers are big fans of all things involving extreme sports, like motocross. We'd like to invite you and Jace on an all-expenses-paid Christmas vacation at a gorgeous lodge in Cheer, Texas."

"There's a Cheer, Texas?" I ask, unable to focus on the rest of what she said. "That's a weird name for a town."

Angel chuckles. "Technically, it's not a real town. It's a massive, multi-million dollar resort-style lodge that looks like a Christmas town. It's Christmas themed all year long, and right now when it's actually December, the resort fills up. These spots are quite coveted and hard to get, and we're offering you and your husband a vacation to remember."

"Just me and Jace, or can our son come, too?"

"This is a couple's vacation," Angel says. "So unfortunately your adorable little boy wouldn't be able to come, but perhaps for season two we could arrange a more family episode."

"Wait, what?" I say, looking up from the notepad I'd been doodling on. "Episode?"

"Oh, sorry, did I not mention that? This vacation would be filmed for our upcoming TV show. Each episode is based on a famous couple from an extreme sport."

"So you're asking us to be on a reality TV show in a fake Christmas town? I barely like putting my face on social media, so being on a TV show sounds... really weird."

"We very much hope you'll accept our offer," Angel says. I can practically feel her huge smile through the phone. I wonder if she's really that happy or if she's trying her hardest to convince me. "Plus, you haven't even heard the best part."

"What's the best part?" I ask, watching as one of my favorite employees, Deja, walks out from her office and refills her coffee mug. She smiles at me and I wave back.

"We'll be paying you fifty thousand dollars."

"Whoa."

"Yep," Angel says. "An all-expenses-paid three-day vacation at a beautiful Christmas resort and you are being paid very well for your time, all in exchange for being on an episode of our show. You'll barely even notice the cameras are there. What do you say?"

I look out the front windows, which face Becca's house. But it doesn't matter that I can't see my backyard right now because I can picture it in my mind. I've been saying for months now that I want a swimming pool in our backyard. Pools are expensive, especially if they have a built-in hot tub like I want. Fifty thousand dollars would pay for a nice pool.

"Let me talk to my husband and I'll call you back."

I write down Angel's phone number and then try to stay patient while Jace gives motocross lessons to one of his regular clients. I want to run outside and interrupt him and tell him about the offer we just got, but I also don't want to be rude to his client. So I sit here and wait. When Becca arrives, I bite the inside of my lip. She's my best friend, but I also want to tell Jace about this first, so I have to hold my tongue.

She's wearing black skinny jeans and a long-sleeved green sweatshirt with sparkly snowflakes all over it. Becca has really leaned into wearing "ugly" Christmas sweaters at work, but they're actually cute on her. I don't think I could pull off that nerdy yet cute look quite as well as my best friend can. She's effortlessly chic.

"How was the dentist?" I ask.

"No cavities!" she says, holding up her hands in celebration. "It's too bad they don't give you a sticker when you're an adult at the dentist," she says with a laugh. "I always loved getting stickers as a kid."

I pull open the drawer under the front desk and grab a stack of address labels someone sent us free in the mail, peeling one off. I stick it to the top of her hand. "There you go. A sticker for a job well done."

Becca laughs. "Thank you very much! So how has work been this morning? Hopefully not too busy?"

"It's not bad. Just a regular day," I say, tapping my fingers on the countertop. I want to talk about the TV show offer *so bad*, but I don't want to tell anyone until Jace knows first.

"Oh, I forgot to tell you—" Becca claps her hands together in front of her chest. "I found that...dirtbike shirt," she says, whispering the last words, "that Jett wanted for Christmas!"

"No way! Where was it?" He's about to turn six on Christmas Eve, but my son has a strong love of motocross, just like his dad. He saw a T-shirt in a motocross magazine a few months ago and he begged me to get it for him, but the website in the magazine ad is all sold out.

Becca pretends to zip her lips closed. "It's a secret."

"Why?" I say, playfully pushing her arm. I technically can't get upset at her keeping secrets because here I am keeping a TV show secret from her. But still… "I wanna know!"

"Nope." She wiggles her eyebrows. "I can't tell you, because Aunty Becca is getting this for my little man, so I'll get all the credit for getting his favorite Christmas gift."

I snort out a laugh. "Fine with me. So long as he gets that freaking shirt, I'm a happy mama."

Jace walks through the front door and I almost trip over myself, completely dropping the conversation with Becca. "Babe! I need to talk to you!"

Jace's brows pull together. "Is everything okay?"

"It's fine. Totally fine, but can we go to your office like, right now?"

"Damn, Bay," Becca says, folding her arms across her chest. "Now I am dying to know what's got you all excited."

I know I'm grinning like an idiot, but I can't help myself. "I'll tell you everything in a minute. I gotta tell Jace first, though."

My husband tilts his head. "Well, this is interesting," he says, exchanging a look with Becca. He holds out his hand toward the hallway. "Let's go to my office."

As soon as the office door closes, I spin around and grin widely. "I just got the coolest phone call."

Jace puts his hands on my hips, pulling me in for a quick kiss. "What's up?"

I tell him about the conversation, and the offer, and the fifty-freaking-thousand dollars.

"Whoa," he says, scratching the back of his neck. He sits on the corner of his desk, while I stand here in front of him bouncing on my toes with excitement. "That's a lot of money for one TV episode. What was the point of the show?"

"What do you mean?" I ask.

"Reality TV shows always have some point... like a baking competition or trying to remodel a house or something. They just want us to go to a Christmas resort for no reason?"

I shrug. "That's what she said."

"There has to be some kind of catch..."

"It's fifty thousand dollars, babe. We could build a pool with that money. We'd have to find a babysitter for Jett, but I'm sure Becca wouldn't mind..."

He nods. "True. Do you want to do it?"

I bite my lip. "Do *you* want to do it?"

"We've been working pretty hard these last few years... getting the business up and running, fixing up our new house...I think we could use a vacation."

I walk up, moving to stand between his knees

while he sits on the corner of his desk. I put my hands on his chest. "Are you saying yes?"

He wraps his hands around me, pulling me closer. He just got back from giving a lesson outside so he smells a little earthy, and slightly like exhaust fumes and motor oil. It's a good smell on him. It smells like home.

I love kissing my husband, don't get me wrong. He's really good at it. Even after all these years, being this close to him still sets off butterflies in my stomach. But right now, I keep the kiss short. I look into his eyes. "Well... are we doing this?"

"I want to do whatever you want to do," he says, giving me that crooked grin of his.

This time I kiss him a little bit longer.

"Let's do it."

AFTER A FEW PHONE CONVERSATIONS AND SOME SIGNED contracts, Jace and I are ready to go on our reality TV adventure. It's a Christmas-themed episode, but it will take place two weeks before Christmas so they have time to edit the episode and air it before Christmas Day. We definitely wouldn't have taken this opportunity if it had been on the actual holiday because we'd never leave Jett on Christmas. Not even for fifty grand.

Angel said the film crew will meet us at The Track instead of our house next door because it will appeal to the motocross fans to see us at our business. That's fine with us, because it's not exactly a secret that we live next door to our business, but it's also a good idea not to film inside our house in case any obsessive fans get any ideas. So at nine in the morning, Jace and I load up our suitcases and step outside.

It's not even that cold out here, thanks to Texas weather, and normally I'm fine with that, but it's a little disappointing to be going on a holiday vacation to a town that's focused on the winter season and it doesn't even feel much like winter. I remind myself that this trip is both free and comes with a huge paycheck, so I really shouldn't complain about the weather. It's not like it's going to snow or anything. It rarely ever snows in Texas.

"Mommy, I'll carry your suitcase," Jett says, reaching for the handle of my rolling bag.

"I don't know, honey, it's pretty heavy," I say. "Plus, you already have your backpack!"

"My backpack is on my back," he says, holding up his hands to demonstrate that his hands are free. "My hands are empty."

Jace chuckles. "He's got a point."

"I'm strong." Jett takes my suitcase and rolls it down the driveway. By the time we get to the grass that cuts across to The Track, he's struggling a bit to roll the suitcase over the uneven terrain, but he still refuses to let me help him.

"He's like a mini you," I whisper to Jace.

Jace grins back. "I raised him well."

Becca and Park are already at The Track, having opened the business for the day. Becca is excited that we're going to be on a reality TV show but Park isn't convinced. When we told them what we're doing, Park kept shaking his head and saying things like, "I don't know, man. Reality TV is pretty brutal."

Despite his objections, they happily agreed to watch Jett for us. Becca doesn't talk about it too much, but she really wants kids of her own. She and Park have tried for years, and will probably keep trying until they get pregnant. She loves kids, and she really loves Jett, so when I ask her to watch after him, she's always happy to do it. This time, she's thrilled that he'll spend a few days at their house.

We hang out in the front lobby for just a few minutes, because the TV crew arrives right on schedule. They're in a large black box van that doesn't have any logos or anything on the outside. A crew of two women and two men pile out of the van. The men are holding cameras on their shoulders. The moment I see the cameras, my stomach tightens into a nervous knot.

"Are we really doing this?" I say in a voice quiet enough that only Jace can hear. He slides an arm sound my waist.

"Guess we are," he says, wiggling his eyebrows mischievously at me. Jace has been in front of a camera much more than I ever have. He's been doing interviews at motocross tracks since he was a teenager. I guess this is no big deal to him.

Angel is the first person through the door and she's all smiles. She looks like she's in her twenties, probably around our age, and she's wearing black leather pants and knee high boots with a purple sweater. She's definitely dressed for cold weather. I'm betting she's not from Texas.

"It's so lovely to meet you," she says, shaking Jace's hand and then mine. "Oh, don't worry about them," she says when she sees me staring at the camera men. "Cameras aren't on for this part."

"When this light is blinking," one guy says, tapping the front of his camera, "you'll know I'm recording you."

I nod, trying to hide the nerves in my stomach. "Cool."

This is supposed to be a fun, carefree adventure. But suddenly I feel really awkward. Especially since I look like a regular person and Angel looks like a superstar. It must have taken hours to do her hair and makeup this morning. If they film both of us standing together, I'll look like some small town troll.

Angel introduces us to the cameramen, whose names are Ricky and Jack—but I don't remember which name goes with which man. The other woman with her is her assistant, and she doesn't bother telling me the woman's name. In fact, Angel barely even acknowledges that her assistant is in the room until she needs something and then she barks the order and the poor lady rushes to do exactly as she's told.

Showbiz. It's a weird biz.

"Okay, so here's what we're going to do," Angel says. Her eyes are alight with adventure as she surveys the room. "I want you here," she says, moving me to the front counter where I usually stand when I'm working. "And I want you over here." She moves Jace to the barstool that's next to me.

Then she looks at Becca and Park. "And can you two go in the other room? Should we have the kid out here or make him come in later?"

The camera guys join in and soon they're looking all over the office, trying to stage the perfect places we all should be located for when they come in and start filming. Angel tells us they'll pretend to surprise us by walking into the lobby and announcing that they're whisking us away on a Christmas vacation. We're supposed to pretend that we never heard of this and had no idea it was happening ahead of time.

"I thought this was a reality show?" Jace says after his "starting position" has been moved three times. Now, instead of standing next to me behind the front counter, they want him standing near the doors hanging up Christmas garland. We have decorations here at The Track, but Angel brought her own garland.

"It is reality, darling," Angel says, flashing a smile that feels as fake as this reality TV setup.

He lifts an eyebrow. Angel just snorts. "All reality TV is scripted just a teensy bit."

She winks at us and then turns her attention to my son, who has been standing in the hallway with Park and Becca.

"Hi there," she says in a sweet child-like voice. "Are you super sad that your mommy and daddy are leaving you?"

"No," Jett says.

Angel frowns. "You're not just a little bit sad? They're going really far away. You'll be here without them."

Jett looks at me and then his dad, and then back to Angel and shrugs. "I'll still be here at my home with Park and Becca, so it's not sad. They're coming back home in a few days."

I can't help but grin. If I had thought for one moment that my son would be upset that we were leaving, I wouldn't have been able to go. But Jett loves Park and Becca—they're like his second set of parents, and they live next door. He doesn't mind one bit that we're leaving. In fact, he probably loves it because his second set of parents spoil him rotten. They'll probably order him pizza and a hot fudge sundae and let him eat it in bed while watching cartoons way past his bedtime. Frankly, I'm surprised Jett isn't pushing us out the door.

Angel is not impressed. She frowns and looks pretty annoyed, then turns back to her camera crew. "Well, I guess we won't get the sad crying kit shot. Oh well—let's get in places and get this show on the road."

She snaps her fingers and everyone falls into place. Most of the crew walks outside, except for one guy who positions himself in the far back corner, I guess to be able to film Angel walking inside. I see the red light turn on, and a shiver of excitement and nervousness rips through me. Outside, the other cameraman turns his camera on and Angel talks to it, moving her hands around while she sets the scene. I imagine she's doing that thing that reality TV show hosts do when they tell the audience what's about to happen. I'm standing at the front counter, staring at the work computer, hands on the keyboard pretending to do real work. With each second that passes, I get more nervous.

Then, she's walking toward the door. It opens. The two camera guys walk in after her. Everything that happens next is a blur.

She talks animatedly as she "surprises" us with the news that we've been chosen to go on a romantic all-expenses-paid Christmas vacation. My dear husband is a fantastic actor. He actually looks surprised, and then walks over to me and puts his arm around my shoulder.

"This seems like a fun adventure," he tells me, using the line Angel had told him to say earlier. "What do you say, babe?"

I hesitate for just a second because I can't remember my line. Angel had told me to say something cutesy and fun, but crap—I'm drawing a blank. I smile up at Jace and nod. "I'd love to!"

It must be fine, though, because Angel stays into character and whisks us outside, where a massive white Hummer limousine is waiting. I didn't even see the thing pull up; I guess I was too nervous about the cameras. It's a huge vehicle, all boxy and imposing. Angel opens the door for us and we climb inside. She says some stuff to the camera, waves goodbye, and shuts the door.

I exhale, eyes wide as I turn to Jace.

"Whoa. That was crazy."

"Tell me about it," he says, shaking his head.

I run my fingers over the smooth black leather interior. "This limo is insane."

"Hi there!" a voice calls out from the front of the limo. It startles both of us. The man is middle-aged with dark short hair and light brown skin. He smiles at us in the rearview mirror. "Your destination is about three hours away, so get comfortable."

"What about our stuff?" I ask, looking out the window. "We need to get our suitcases and—"

"It's all taken care of, ma'am," the guy says.

Right. Okay.

Jace wraps his arm around me and I snuggle up against him. The limo seats actually recline, and there's even a little TV in here. We get comfortable and I'm about to tell him how crazy this is, but then I see it—a tiny little red light up in the corner of the limo.

We're being recorded.

"I see it, too," he whispers.

"This is weird," I whisper back.

He nods, his lips sliding to the side of his mouth. "Although, when you think about it, TV shows are only like half an hour long. So if they record us the whole week, they'll only use a small bit of the footage. I doubt there's anything worth using of us just sitting in a limo, ya know?"

"True…" I look over at the camera again, and I'm reminded of something Angel had told us. She'd said not to worry about the cameras. She told us not to look directly at them, because it ruins the TV show aspect of it. We're supposed to be living our lives and pretending like it's all realistic and that we aren't being filmed.

I take a deep breath, wondering what I got myself into. Jace seems fine, though.

Think of the money, I remind myself. *Think of the pool we'll get when this is all over.*

Then I close my eyes and snuggle up against my husband and fall asleep.

When Jace softly wakes me up a few hours later, I peer out the window.

We are in a winter wonderland.

THERE MIGHT NOT BE ANY SNOW ON THE GROUND, BUT Cheer, Texas doesn't need it. The limo driver takes us slowly down Main Street, either because it has a slow speed limit or maybe just so we can see the sights. The street has two lanes of traffic going each way plus a large sidewalk on the side. Both sides of the road are filled with old-timey shops. They're all absolutely covered in Christmas lights and green garlands. The most beautiful part is the multiple green leafy garlands that stretch across the road, suspended on thin cables. They're wrapped in clear Christmas lights with big red bows in the center. Everything is stunning.

Suddenly I want to go home and decorate my house. It's already decorated, and our Christmas tree is up, but it's nothing like this. This town makes me feel wrapped in a Christmas blanket. I want my home to feel that way, too.

At the end of the street, the road turns to the left and Jace and I watch in awe as the limo driver takes us to the Cheer Lodge, a rustic-looking three story hotel that sits on top of a small hill that overlooks the town. The limo slows to a stop, which is well before we arrive at the lodge's guest entrance.

"The mayor wants to meet you," our driver calls back to us. It's such a long car you kind of have to yell to hear each other.

That's when we notice a portly, middle-aged man wearing red pants and a red and white striped blazer walking up to us. He has a head of thick white hair, but his beard is merely scruffy, not a full Santa beard. Still, the impression he's trying to make isn't lost on me.

Jace opens the door and holds out his hand to help me climb out of the massive car.

"Well, hello there!" the man says. A cameraman stands behind him, filming this whole thing.

Movement to my right catches my attention and I glance over, seeing the other cameraman filming from another angle. Great. I suck in my stomach a little bit. They say the camera adds ten pounds, right? The last thing I need is more of Jace's fans making fun of me online and saying he married the wrong person.

"I'm Mayor Festivus," the man says as he shakes our hands. "And you must be our honored guests, Mr. and Mrs. Adams. I'm so glad to meet you."

"Mayor Festivus, huh?" I don't mean to sound so sarcastic, but I can't help it. The words just tumble out of me.

The mayor lets out a jolly laugh, which I am certain he's practiced so that it sounds just like Santa Claus. "Yes, ma'am," he says, winking at me. "When you love Christmas as much as I do, you legally change your name."

"That's amazing," I say, flashing him a smile so he doesn't think I'm rude. And honestly, I'm not trying to be rude. I just feel really on edge with these cameras watching my every move. Jace had a good point when he said they'd be editing down the footage into a half-hour episode, but I'm pretty sure the "meeting the mayor" scene will be part of the show, so I feel nervous and weird inside. If cameramen are going to follow me around the whole time, the least they could do is also hold up a mirror so I can check my reflection to make sure I don't look stupid.

"It's nice to meet you, sir," Jace says, saving me from awkward conversation. "You have a beautiful town."

"This town is all yours to enjoy," he says, sweeping out his hand. "We'll get your bags taken to the lodge, and for now, why don't you two lovebirds get acquainted with Cheer, Texas?"

The small Christmas-themed town appears to be completely walkable. It's just Main Street, which has beautiful stories lining both sides of the street for about five blocks, and then everything beyond looks like a few homes, and maybe a museum or two. It's almost like these people just took a large piece of land and turned it into a magical, Stars-Hollow-esque town that looks like Christmas all year long. It's kind of awesome and also a tiny bit... creepy? I dunno how exactly I feel about this odd little town. But I dig it for now.

There's definitely no way I'd ever want to live in a town like this all year round. I like Christmas and all, but I also like summer. And Halloween. And spring.

The limo drives off toward the lodge and the mayor walks with us for a little bit, telling us all about the history of this town. He proudly boasts that he's been mayor since day one, which was four years ago. The cameras follow us on this quaint little walk along the sidewalk. One guy in front of us and one behind. I know I'm supposed to ignore them, but it's really hard to ignore the big piece of machinery sitting on some guy's shoulder.

We approach the first shop to our right. It's called "A Little Bit of Christmas" and it's an entire store filled with ornaments.

"Let's go in!" I tell Jace, squeezing his forearm.

"Wonderful choice," Mayor Festivus says in his jovial tone. He waves at us as Jace opens the shop door. "You two have fun, and I'll see you at dinner at the lodge tonight!"

The ornament shop smells like cinnamon and nutmeg. Cheerful Christmas music plays from hidden speakers overhead. Every single inch of the place is filled with every possible ornament design you can imagine. Instead of racks or shelves to display the merchandise, the store has dozens of artificial Christmas trees filled with the ornaments. Glitter ornaments, glass, plastic, metal, wood. Every single hobby and profession are represented here. There's ornaments that look like nail polish bottles, soccer balls, books—a stethoscope. Everything you could ever want is here.

Jace and I hold hands and wander through the

trees, looking at all the beautiful ornaments. One tree is filled with souvenir ornaments that say Cheer, TX. I pick one out to take home with us.

"Hey, look!" Jace says, reaching for an ornament hanging high up in a tree. It's a dirt bike.

"We have to get that for Jett!" I say, taking the ornament to admire it. "We should get something for everyone in our family."

A young woman with long black hair walks up to us. She's wearing a red and white dress that's fashioned like a feminine version of a Santa suit, with white fur lining around the hem of the skirt and around her wrists. She holds out a hand basket. "Hello, ma'am. Would you like this shopping basket to hold all your items?"

"Yes, that's perfect," I say, taking it and carefully placing the dirt bike ornament inside. "Thank you."

"You're so welcome," she says with a warm smile. Then her eyes drift over to Jace and her mouth falls open. "Oh. My. God," she says, eyes wide. "Are you Jace Adams?"

Jace's ear twitches. It happens every time someone recognizes him when he's not expecting it. When he's at a motocross race, he knows fans will come up and want to snap a selfie with him or ask for his autograph. He's prepared for times like that.

But right now, he's not and it catches him off-guard.

"Um," he says. Before he can get another word out, the woman squeals.

"It is you! *Ohmygod!* I'm such a huge fan." She bounces on her toes and rushes up to him, squeezing him in a tight hug. "You're, like, my favorite motocross racer ever."

"Thanks," he says, taking a step backward.

She doesn't notice his silent request for more space though, because she takes another step toward him. She presses her hands to his chest and then squeezes his bicep. "You're really sexy, you know that? I could tell you were muscular from your photos but, wow!"

Jace wriggles out of her grasp and flashes me a look that says *help*. But I'm not exactly sure what to do because there's a camera on me and I don't want to say something rude and then have it talked about online later.

The woman just can't seem to keep her hands off him. She tries reaching for his hair. He takes her wrists and pushes them down. "Excuse me, but I'm here shopping with my wife."

She turns around to me and giggles like she only just noticed I exist, despite giving me this basket just a moment ago. "Oh, sorry!" she says, turning back to Jace and giving him the most flirty look I've ever seen. "You know where to find me if you ever want to give me a call." She winks at him and then saunters away.

Jace puts a hand on his chest and gives me a wide-eyed look. "That was gross."

I laugh. "Yeah... she was very into you."

He peers around a Christmas tree, noting that another person is working the cash register. "Let's buy these and get the heck out of here."

As we're walking out of the store, Angel (and a cameraman) are waiting for us just outside.

"We're going to do a talking head," she says, motioning for the camera guy to move over to the left a bit. "That means you talk to the camera and we'll splice in your commentary throughout the show. I'll ask you questions, but just answer the camera, not me. Got it?"

I nod.

"Sure thing," Jace says, running a hand through his hair.

Angel turns to me. "That woman really seemed to like Jace. Doesn't that just piss you off?"

I start to talk but she nods toward the camera, so I look at the big camera lens instead. "Not really."

Angel sighs. "Sorry, hon. I need you to talk in complete sentences so the audience knows what you're talking about. Rephrase my question, but as an answer."

"Right…" I say with a nod. Angel smiles and snaps her fingers, pointing toward the camera. I try not to think about the blinking red light on top of it.

"I'm used to women hitting on Jace when we're out in public," I say with a shrug. "So that woman didn't bother me. If anything, I think she embarrassed herself."

"Don't you ever get jealous?" Angel asks.

I look at the camera. "I guess I got a little jealous of that kind of stuff years ago, but not anymore. Jace and I are soul mates, and I don't really care if other women want him."

I loop my arm around his elbow and smile up at him. "He's mine."

Chapter Five

WITH OUR ORNAMENTS IN TOW, JACE AND I DECIDE TO check into our hotel room before we walk around the rest of the town. Mostly because I have to pee, but also because it feels weird not having seen our room yet when we're going to be spending a few nights here. Also, I'd like a little break from the cameras.

The lodge is stunning from the outside, but the moment we walk inside, we're both in awe. Most of the walls are made of wood paneling with stone facades and high ceilings. Christmas decorations are abundant but they look so elegant here and not crowded or overdone. It's almost like the architect designed this place specifically to be a holiday wonderland.

We check in at the front desk and a man wearing a navy blue tuxedo takes us to our room on the third floor. Jace and I hold hands, but I don't say a word because the cameras are watching. The elevator plays Christmas carols instead of elevator music, and when the elevator opens on the third floor, we're treated to a hallway lined with Christmas trees that are just as ornate as the ones from the ornament shop.

The usher leads us to our room, which is at the end of the hall.

"Apologies for the long walk," he says, tapping a plastic key card to the door, "But this room has the best view of the entire lodge. It's at the end of the building so the windows wrap around two walls."

We walk inside.

"Wow, you weren't kidding," Jace tells him.

"This is stunning," I say. My hand slips from Jace's as I walk further into the room, checking everything out. The room is massive. It's really what you'd call a suite, now that I think about it. Plus it smells delightfully like Christmas. Every breath I take fills me with joy. I can't quite put my finger on it —cinnamon, maybe, and fir. And something that smells distinctly like Christmas.

The walls are wooden with log rafters bracing

the high ceiling. Large floor-to-ceiling windows span across two walls, giving us a beautiful view of the small town below. Leather couches fill the seating area along with an incredible Christmas tree that has to be at least twenty feet tall. A massive chandelier hangs from the center of the tall ceiling. I guess you'd call it a chandelier—it's made from moose antlers and light bulbs. It's not exactly my style but it's rustic and the perfect vibe for the lodge. Plush rugs dot the hardwood floor and I want to kick off my shoes and sink my toes into the carpeting. There's even a large stone fireplace in the middle of the living area with a TV above the mantle.

"The phone is right over there," the man says, pointing to a phone in the small kitchenette area. "Just give us a call if you need anything."

We thank him and he refuses a cash tip when Jace tries to tip him. He tells us the entire trip is being paid for by the television company. And then he leaves, closing the door behind him. But we're not alone.

The two camera guys hang out on opposite sides of the suite. I try to ignore them and venture around the room. Jace and I had a pretty luxurious honeymoon a few years ago, but this room rivals all of the five-star hotels we stayed in back then. This place is incredible. The bedroom area has a king sized bed with a leather headboard, its own Christmas tree in the corner, and one of those cool plush chaise lounge chairs.

I peek into the bathroom but there's a camera guy behind me so I don't go in very far. It feels weird walking into a bathroom—even a luxurious one like this—with some strange man following me, filming the whole thing. We were told the cameras wouldn't follow us into the bathroom, but I guess that only counts for when we're *using* the bathroom, not merely looking inside of it.

I walk back into the main area and find Jace sitting all spread out on the couch, his head tipped back and relaxing while he gazes at the fireplace.

"What do you think?" he asks me.

"I love it," I say, sitting next to him. "I want to come here every year and bring Jett with us."

Jace wraps his arm around my shoulders. "I miss the little man already."

I lean my head on his shoulder and kick my feet up on the coffee table. "Me too."

I'd say more if we were alone, but we're not, and it's awkward. I wonder if Jace feels that way too, but I don't want to ask in front of the cameras. One of the guys walks around slowly, stopping about seven feet in front of us. I try really hard not to look at him or acknowledge his existence, but it's weird.

"Do you think we should call Jett?" I ask.

"Yeah, for sure." Jace takes out his phone and calls Park using the video chat feature. They chat for a minute, and then Park calls for Jett who is in the other room with Becca. He comes running in with a big smile on his face. Our son absolutely loves playing at their house.

Jace holds his phone out so we can both fit into the video screen.

"Hey, little man!" Jace says.

"Hi, daddy!" Jett says, waving.

"What are you up to?" I ask.

"Playing with dough."

"Huh?" I ask, thinking I heard him wrong. Dough is a weird word I'm not expecting him to say.

Beside him Becca says, "Shh... it's a surprise, remember?"

His eyes go wide. "Oops! Nevermind, Mommy!"

I smile, acting like I have no idea what they're talking about, but I remember Becca talking about this flour dough recipe she found online. You use holiday themed cookie cutters and it forms hard cookie-type ornaments that you can bake and then hang up on the tree. They must be making us surprise ornaments.

"You wanna see our hotel room?" Jace asks. Jett nods.

Jace turns the camera around and then walks him around the room, showing off all the cool parts, like the chandelier and the large patio balcony outside. One cameraman follows Jace and the other one stays put near the couch, focused on me.

As soon as we say goodbye and Jace hangs up the phone, there's a knock on our hotel door. I shouldn't be surprised to see Angel standing there, but I am. I guess I thought it would be the same usher from before, or maybe even the mayor, giving us some cookies or something.

Angel walks right into our room without being invited.

"Hey guys," she says, flipping her hair over her shoulder. "I have some unfortunate news."

"What's up?" Jace asks.

"There was a…mixup…and your luggage is lost."

"Huh?" I look at Jace and then back at Angel. "It was literally in the back of the limo."

"Yes, but sadly the limo driver left before we unloaded it, so your luggage is now a hundred miles away."

"It's only been about two hours," Jace says, glancing at his watch. "Can't the guy just turn around and come back and drop it off?"

"Sadly, no." Angel doesn't look very sad. In fact, she looks delighted to be giving us bad news. "The limo was hired for another event so he won't be back for a couple of days. But don't worry, we're making sure your luggage will remain safe, and we'll get it back to you as soon as we can."

"My phone charger was in there. And my makeup, and stuff," I say, frowning.

"I'm sure they sell all of that stuff here in town," Jace says, sliding his arm around me.

"Yes, they certainly do," Angel says.

I shrug and slide my hands into my back pockets. "Well, I guess we're gonna go shopping. We can get new clothes, too. That'll be fun. I love clothes shopping."

"Well, about that…" Angel looks a little too happy, once again. "You might have a problem buying new clothes…"

"Surely there are clothes here," I say, motioning toward the window which overlooks the town. "There are a ton of stores."

"Oh yes, they have clothes." Angel smiles. "Unfortunately, they're all Christmas themed."

EVERYTHING IN CHEER, TEXAS IS CHRISTMAS THEMED. Even the phone chargers, which we pick up in the souvenir shop inside the hotel, along with tooth-paste and toothbrushes and a big bottle of shampoo and conditioner because I use a lot more conditioner than the tiny bottles that hotels have. After drop-ping off that stuff in our room, we venture back out to the town.

"It's a beautiful day," I say, looking up at the clear blue sky. It's a little chilly, but not cold, and it's not too humid like it gets in the summers. "Except for the fact that cameras are following us and all our stuff is gone, this is a really beautiful day."

"Every day I'm with you is a beautiful day," Jace says.

I roll my eyes. He's probably just saying that because the cameras are watching us, but it still makes me blush anyway. Now that it's mid-afternoon, the town has more people outside, shopping and hanging out. We pass a few restaurants and cafes with indoor and outdoor seating, both of which are mostly full. Main Street is hustling and bustling right now, even though barely anyone was here when we were out here just an hour ago. Curiosity makes me wonder if the TV show has something to do with this. I glance at the people as we pass them. Are they actors? Paid extras that hang out in the background? Or am I just being paranoid?

It doesn't matter, I decide. We're getting paid fifty grand for doing this little TV episode, so it's totally worth it.

"This looks like a clothing shop," Jace says, pulling me out of my thoughts. We stop in front of a place called Season's Greetings Boutique. The large windows are painted with green wreaths and snowflakes, but beyond them are racks and racks of clothing.

"Let's do this," I say, leading the way inside.

Angel wasn't kidding. This boutique has everything you could need, from pajamas to swimwear, to loungewear, and even some cocktail dresses. Every single thing—even the underwear and bras—are red and green, or blue and silver, with holly or snowflakes or big Santa faces on it. It's all Christmas. It's gaudy and tacky in the most delightful way.

I load up Jace's arms with clothes, choosing way more things than we'd even need for the next few days. I can't help myself though. It's all adorable.

"Do you really need five ugly Christmas sweaters?" Jace asks, grinning at me as I toss another one over his outstretched arms.

"It's just four ugly Christmas sweaters," I say, lifting up on my toes to kiss his cheek. "This one is a sweater dress. It's totally different."

"It doesn't look any different," he says, peering at it.

"It's longer. It's a dress."

"Ah, so I'll get to see your sexy legs in it?" He nods approvingly. "Let's buy more sweater dresses."

"Can do!" I say with a laugh as I go searching for more things to get. Jace has never been big on buying himself stuff, so I do most of the shopping for him. Honestly, it's one of the perks of being married. I love finding things for him to wear.

I grab him a pair of jeans that have candy canes embroidered on the back pockets, some boxers covered in snowmen and present graphics, and a couple pairs of flannel pajamas. Nothing in this store is subtle. It's not just a simple red and green plaid flannel. It's plaid flannel with reindeer on it, or the words HoHoHo or Merry Christmas scrawled across the front.

"It's like a whole different culture here," I say, finding a T-shirt that actually lights up if you press a little button on the collar. "We might as well look like we belong while we're here."

"That shirt looks too small for me," Jace says. I hold it up to him and tilt my head.

"We need to find a fitting room."

We venture through the store, which has filled up with customers after we got in here, and find the fitting rooms at the back. I toss all of the clothes I picked out for Jace into one stall and toss mine into the other.

"Aww, that's no fair," Jace says, frowning.

"What?" I say.

He wiggles his eyebrows suggestively. "We should use the same room," he says, running a hand down my arm. A thrilling little zap of electricity shoots through my body.

"That sounds fun but..." I look around. This is a small shop and there are at least thirty people in here, including a fierce-looking little old lady working the register. Not to mention the camera. "People might see us," I whisper to him.

There's a camera so close I could reach out and touch it, so I'm pretty sure they're recording this conversation, but at least that little old lady can't hear what we're saying.

"They don't have to know anything," Jace whispers back. He takes my hand, then he looks out toward the front of the store. "Oh shit, what's that?" he calls out, pointing.

The cameraman swings around and Jace pulls me into the fitting room, closing the door quickly. "Now you're all mine," he whispers, leaning in and kissing my neck.

I close my eyes, unable to resist his touch. A little gasp escapes my lips as he works his magic, kissing down to my collarbone, his hands warm and tight around my back.

My hands tangle up in his hair and I pull him closer to me, kissing him harder. I hadn't realized how much I missed being this close to my husband until we were close again. I want every inch of him, right now.

And then I notice it.

Peeking over the top of the fitting room stall.

Totally killing the mood.

I step away, pushing Jace back a couple of inches. "We have an audience."

Jace turns around. "Dude! Not cool," he says to the camera.

But the camera doesn't move. It doesn't back away and give us privacy. Nope, it just keeps watching us from over the top of the small door in the fitting room stall. Our contract had only stated we get privacy in the bathroom or when changing clothes. We technically aren't changing clothes right now, so they can film us all they like.

I groan and roll my eyes. "Okay, maybe we should really try on this stuff before we buy it."

"Your wish is my command," Jace says, kissing my forehead.

I leave the stall and walk into the next one. Before I close the door, I point a finger at the camera. Who cares if we're not supposed to acknowledge them? This is important.

"If you film me changing clothes I will sue the crap out of you," I say, giving them a warning glare. The contract we'd signed was pretty clear.

I keep my eyes focused on the door, but they don't try to film me as I try on some of the clothes, and after a few minutes, I can relax.

Jace walks out in his candy cane skinny jeans and does a little fashion walk for me. "These are so tacky," he says, curling his lip.

"I love them."

"There's no way you like these pants."

I grin. "Oh, I do. Your butt looks very cute with candy canes on it."

Jace laughs. "My guy friends are going to give me so much shit for this."

I shrug. "Who cares? They don't have a TV show and we do."

Jace holds out his fist and bumps it to mine in solidarity. "Good point."

We spend the next hour trying on our clothes and modeling for each other. I put on my sweater dress and do a playful little dance for him while he sits in a leather armchair just outside of the fitting rooms. I am fully aware that the cameras are watching, but you know who else will be watching? All the women who tell me Jace is too good for me and should marry someone else.

The way Jace fawns over me and compliments each outfit I choose shows that he loves me, and only me. I think we put on a pretty fun little fashion show for the cameras, and I'm confident they'll show this when our episode airs. What can I say? I am feeling myself with these holiday-themed outfits.

We get at least a week's worth of outfits, plus underwear and pajamas, even though we are only staying for three days. Jace also insists on getting swimsuits since the hotel has a heated indoor pool. He gets swim trunks that look like Santa's pants and I get a Mrs. Claus-themed bikini.

We carry all of our purchases up to the register and then wait patiently while the clerk rings them up. Jace keeps flirting with me while we wait in line, and I can tell people are watching. I keep waiting for someone to run up and ask for a picture with him or something, but nothing happens.

Once all of our items are rung up, Jace hands over his credit card to the clerk. She swipes it and the machine makes an angry noise. She swipes it again, only to get the same noise.

"This card is declined," she says, peering at both of us through flat lips.

"That doesn't make any sense," Jace says. "We just bought phone chargers with that card."

The lady shrugs.

Jace takes out another card from his wallet. "Try this one."

The machine beeps again.

"If you can't afford to buy all of these items, you need to leave," the woman says. The couple standing in line behind us mutters impatiently.

"This is taking forever," one of them says.

"I can afford this," Jace says. I love how he never gets rude with people who are rude to him in situations like this. "Maybe your machine is messed up. Can you restart it?"

"My machine works perfectly fine," the woman says, tossing both of the credit cards back at him. "You out-of-towners always come here thinking you can take advantage of our small town."

"Ma'am, that's not true—" Jace says.

"Did you think I'd just give you all of this for free?" the woman says, her voice getting louder with each word. "That's not how this works! I don't care that you have a TV show following you around. You will pay for these things or you will leave!"

"Do you take Venmo?" I ask. "Or PayPal?"

She purses her lips and folds her arms across her chest. "We take cash and credit cards only."

"Wait, I have cash," Jace says, opening his wallet again. He reaches into one of the credit card slots and pulls out folded up cash. "I always keep this for emergencies." He unfolds four hundred dollar bills and puts them on the counter. The total amount was only three hundred and twenty dollars, but Jace flashes the rude lady his brightest smile and says, "Keep the change."

"You're such a badass," I say once we're outside with our shopping bags in tow.

"How so?" he asks.

"That lady was super rude, but you handled it so well. I wanted to cuss her out."

He chuckles. "I did, too but I'm pretty sure that little fiasco was set up, if you know what I mean."

He whispers that last part and I lean in closer to him while we walk. "What do you mean?"

His head nods slightly toward the cameraman in front of us—a quick gesture that I notice but no one else would. "My credit cards have a zero balance and high credit limits. They work."

"Ah..." I nod. It's Reality TV. And there's always drama in Reality TV. But I don't say that out loud since we're being filmed. "I think Park was on to something," I say instead.

Jace nods. "Yup."

"Ooh, hot chocolate!" I point to the little drink cart on the side of the road. It has a red and white little umbrella shielding the owner from the elements. The chalkboard sign on the ground next to him says that the hot chocolate is made from real

Belgian chocolate and there are different flavors to choose from. Vanilla, hazelnut, dark chocolate, milk chocolate, and cinnamon.

"Looks delicious," Jace says.

We step into the short line and when it's our turn, Jace hands over his credit card.

It works perfectly.

The man hands us our drinks and Jace smirks as he slides his credit card back into his wallet. "Park was totally right."

Back at our hotel, Jace and I meet up in the bathroom where the cameras aren't allowed. I turn on the shower just so it makes noise. I wouldn't put it past them to put a listening device near the bathroom door to catch us talking.

In the privacy of the large bathroom, Jace leans against the counter and I lean against him, my arms around his neck.

"Okay, so..." I say playfully. "We are definitely on a reality TV show where they are trying to create drama."

He nods and slides his hands down over my butt. "I'm starting to think that crazy fan we met when we got here was a plant, too. And losing our luggage was totally done on purpose. I bet our stuff is actually here somewhere in a closet and not still on that limo."

"Why would they do such silly things?" I say softly, keeping my voice quiet enough so that only Jace can hear.

He shrugs. "I guess we're not that exciting on our own. They want to spice things up."

"We know how to spice things up," I whisper as I playfully bite his lip.

He squeezes me tighter. "That shower is totally big enough for two…"

I give him a mischievous grin and then pull off my shirt and walk over to the large shower that's already steamy from the hot water. "Let's go, Adams."

WHEN WE EMERGE from our shower, only one cameraman is present. He's not even holding the camera. I guess he chose to get a little break himself since we were in a room he wasn't allowed to film. He's sitting on the barstool in the kitchenette, playing on his phone. The large camera sits on the counter, and I'm relieved to see the red blinking light turned off for once.

He looks up sheepishly as we walk out.

"Where's the other guy?" Jace asks. He grabs an apple from the fruit bowl on the counter and takes a bite.

"He's off for the night. I'm supposed to stay until midnight and then I'll head out and you'll finally get some privacy."

"Oh, nice," I say, looking at the time on my phone. "Four more hours to go until a tiny bit of freedom."

The camera guy nods. "You'll be alone from midnight until morning each night you're here. Is this your first TV show?"

"Yep," Jace says, biting the apple again. "Unless you count being filmed while racing a dirt bike, which is a whole lot easier if you ask me."

The guy chuckles. "I can tell you guys are newbies. The people who have been on reality TV for a while act a lot differently."

"How so?" I ask.

He picks up the camera and sets it in his lap. "They're... well, they're fake. They put on an act for the camera. You guys aren't like that. You're just nice, normal people."

I smile at Jace and he smiles back at me.

"I should warn you that Angel will be here soon," the guy says. "She'll get a few talking heads of you two before I wrap up for the night."

"Let's eat before she gets here," Jace says, reaching for the room service menu on the end table near the couch. "I'm starving."

"Sorry about this, but I gotta start filming again."

"Just when I was starting to like you," I say sarcastically. He laughs and loads the camera onto his shoulder. That weird ball of anxiety floods into my stomach again. Being filmed is beyond weird.

Room service is delicious. Our dinner is brought right to our door without an incident and Jace and I eat it in front of the television in our room. I was a little worried that they'd bring us the wrong food, or tell us the kitchen was closed or something, and luckily none of that happened.

"They know how to cook dinner in this town," Jace says as he cuts into his steak. "This is insanely good."

"I was afraid the only thing on the menu would be like, candy canes and sugar cookies," I say as I take a bite of my blackened chicken avocado salad. "But this is good. Really good."

"It's the first thing that's gone right today," Jace says with a mouthful of food.

It only takes a few minutes to realize that every single channel on the hotel's television is just a holiday movie channel. All holiday movies, all the time.

"This is so weird," Jace says, flipping through the channels one more time. "It's all Christmas movies."

"Well, I like Christmas movies," I say. Picking up my salad, I slide back on the couch and stretch my legs over onto his lap. With the remote in one hand, Jace rubs my feet with the other hand, and we choose a movie to watch.

It's almost possible to forget that there's a guy sitting in the corner of the room filming everything we do, but then out of the corner of my eye, I'll see that freaking blinking red light and be reminded that we're not alone. I seriously don't know how reality TV stars do it. I'd go crazy if this was my entire life. I like my privacy. I like knowing that if I accidentally say or do something stupid it won't be broadcast on national television where everyone can see it.

I remind myself that I'm doing this for the pool, and the nerves in my stomach settle down a bit.

We get mostly through an entire movie before

there's a knock at the door. Angel wears the same outfit from this morning. She lets herself inside again.

"How's it going?" she asks in this bubbly way like she's a cheerleader coach and we're her teenage students. "Are you just loving this town or what?"

"It's been fun," I say.

"Wonderful."

She flips on lights and finds a spot on the couch that has the best lighting, then directs us to sit on either side of the couch.

"We'll do individual talking heads first, then you can sit closer together and we'll do some talking heads with the both of you."

This time around, it's not so awkward to talk to a camera and answer the things she asks. She brings up the embarrassing credit card snafu, and has us talk about how sad we are that our luggage was lost. The thing is, we're not really that sad about it. I hadn't even packed my laptop for this trip, which is a good thing. I'd be really mad if that was lost.

When I mention the good news that my laptop is safe at home, Angel frowns. "Can you say all of that again, but don't mention your laptop. Try to act sad about missing your luggage. Okay?"

I try not to roll my eyes and remind myself of

the swimming pool we're going to buy with all the money we make from this. And then I look into the camera and try to act sad about losing our luggage.

We do talking heads for over an hour, and *finally* Angel leaves, taking the camera man with her. Jace twists the deadbolt, locking us inside the room and keeping them out. He turns around and lets out a big sigh.

"This was a crazy day."

"We are finally alone!" I sing-song, tossing my hands in the air.

He laughs. "I've never appreciated privacy as much as I do now."

"We can finally act like ourselves again."

"You acted pretty normal," he says, smacking me on the butt as I walk toward the bed.

"Did I? Because I felt like a weirdo all day. I was so hyperfocused on the camera and that stupid blinking light," I say, bursting my fingers out in a blinking motion. "Blink, blink, blink!"

Jace laughs. He pulls down the thick duvet and red satin sheets on our bed. "You weren't a weirdo. Was I a weirdo?"

I shake my head. "You were handsome and sexy all day."

"I don't know if I can trust your opinion...you're a bit biased, after all."

We crawl into bed and I snuggle up against him. "These sheets are fun," I say, sliding my feet around. They're so silky and luxurious. We have cotton sheets at home. They're nice, but not as nice as these.

"We should get sheets like this at home," he agrees. He yawns and wraps his arms around me as I settle on his chest, snuggling close.

"I love you," I say.

"I love you," he replies, kissing the top of my head. "If I'm going to be on a silly reality TV show, I'd only want to be on it with you."

"I wonder what tomorrow will bring," I muse.

He runs a hand through my hair and chuckles. "Guess we'll have to wait and find out."

Chapter Eight

I WAKE UP TO THE SOUND OF BELLS JINGLING. I'M USED TO waking up to weird noises, like the sounds of Jett's battery-powered dirt bike toys, or his video games. I've even been woken up a few times to the sounds of him calling my name from my bedside only to tell me he's sick and just threw up.

But jingle bells? That's a new one.

My eyes flutter open. The noise keeps jingling through the hotel room and after a few moments, I realize it's the sound of the doorbell. I'd seen it when we walked into our hotel room last night, and I remember thinking it was interesting to have a hotel room with a doorbell. Of course this suite is as big as a house, so I guess it makes sense.

I roll over and find my phone on the nightstand. I check the time.

It's six-thirty in the morning!

"Jace," I say groggily as I push on his shoulder. He grunts in reply. "Babe, wake up."

The melodic doorbell keeps going off so whoever is on the other side really wants to see us. Maybe there's a gas leak or an emergency or something. A momentary panic makes me bolt up in bed, hoping our lives aren't in danger. While Jace is yawning and slowly waking up, I run to the door and yank it open, half expecting to see the police or something.

It's the cameraman.

The same guy from last night. I can't even remember his name, and I suddenly feel bad about that.

"Is there an emergency?" I ask him

He's got the camera on his shoulder and the light is on, so I don't expect him to reply since he's supposed to blend into the background while recording us. But he does talk this time. "Good morning. I'm here to film your day."

"It's six in the morning!"

He shrugs. "Filming hours are six a.m. to midnight. I'm a little late this morning though because I forgot to charge the camera batteries."

Jace shuffles over to us, wearing his green and red flannel pajamas. His hair is all messed up and sticking out at odd angles. He yawns. "What's up?"

"We only get six freaking hours of privacy a night," I say, stepping backward to let the cameraman inside. He's just doing his job so I can't really be mad at him.

Jace looks at the camera and then at me. "Is it rude if we go back to bed for a couple of hours? I really don't feel like waking up right now."

"Don't worry about me. You just do your thing and pretend I'm not here."

"Cool," Jace says.

I turn to the camera. "Will you be filming us if we sleep?"

The cameraman moves the camera up and down as if it's the one nodding an answer to us. I roll my eyes. "That is just creepy."

"I don't care," Jace says, yawning again. "Let's get a couple more hours of sleep and then I'll be super entertaining for the camera, I promise."

I follow his lead and crawl back into the massive king sized bed. I pull the covers up really high to my nose to block most of my body. It's not like I'm dressed too revealing or anything, but it's super weird to know that someone is recording me sleeping. What if I snore? Or drool?

The cameraman walks over to the couch and sits down, leaving the camera balanced on his shoulder while he takes out his phone and flips through it. This may be awkward, but I find comfort in knowing that if we don't do anything interesting, it won't be on the TV show. They'll just delete all the boring footage, so who cares?

It's not too hard to fall back asleep. When I wake up again, it's because the phone is ringing. But not my cell phone, and not Jace's. It's the phone on Jace's nightstand, and it should be no surprise that the ringtone is also a Christmas carol. This one is Rockin' Around the Christmas Tree.

Jace sits up and pushes the speakerphone button on the receiver. "Hello?" he says.

"Hi there," the cheerful voice on the other end says. "This is Mrs. Claus calling for the Adams! We have a very special breakfast scheduled this morning and we can't wait to have you as our honored guests." Her voice is so cheerful and grandmotherly that I almost wonder if she really is from the magical fairy-tale land of the North Pole. "Just join us down in the commons area."

"Sure thing," Jace says. "What time?"

"Well, right now, silly! See you soon!"

The call ends. I groan and drape my arm over my eyes. "What time is it now?"

"Seven-thirty," Jace says. He falls back onto the bed and snuggles up to me. "It's so early. Why are they having breakfast *so* early?"

"Do we have to go?" I ask. "Maybe we can just skip it."

Without warning, the hotel door opens. We both jump, sitting up in bed. Angel walks into our hotel suite as if she owns the place. She wears tight black pants with brown knee-high boots and a cream-colored chunky sweater. Her dark hair is pulled up into a loose bun on top of her head.

"Good morning, good morning!" she says, doing a little dance shimmy as she walks up to us. "Are you guys ready for a delicious breakfast with Mrs. Claus?"

Jace turns to me. "To answer your question, my love, I think we do have to go."

THE LODGE'S common area is decorated like some kind of Christmas Hogwarts dining hall. Everything looks vintage and huge and wooden. Instead of floating candles though, there are hundreds of clear Christmas lights strung across the log rafters, casting a beautiful wintery glow down on the long dining table. Waiters line up along the wall, ready to serve. They're wearing red button-up shirts under their black tuxedos and little green bow ties.

And right there, at the head of the long table, is Mrs. Claus. Her red and white fur dress is gorgeous. It looks like something a Disney character would wear at Disney World. Her makeup is flawless and her white hair is piled expertly on top of her head. I've always imagined Mrs. Claus as an older, grandmotherly type of woman, but this woman isn't old at all. She's maybe in her mid-forties, and her smile reminds me of my mom.

I know she's just a woman playing a character right now, but I don't know what else to call her, so I call her Mrs. Claus when I thank her for inviting us to breakfast. I'm still pretty tired, but the huge breakfast buffet in the corner of the room is calling to me. It looks delicious.

As we get our plates and load it up with food, more guests arrive. Most of them are in holiday pajamas like we are, and it almost feels like we're some kind of huge extended family.

A woman taps Jace on the shoulder.

"Are you Jace Adams?" she says, beaming up at him.

He grabs the tongs and loads bacon strips onto his plate. "That's me."

She wraps her hand around his bicep and squeezes. "I'm a huge fan. Would you mind taking a photo with me?"

"Uh, sure," Jace says. He moves to take a selfie with her, but she bites her lip instead.

"Would you mind taking the photo?" she says, holding out her phone to me.

I hold up the woman's phone and fix them in the frame. She wraps both arms around Jace's waist and leans in close, pressing her head against his chest. I resist the urge to roll my eyes and I snap a photo for her.

To her credit, she does thank me before rushing off to her seat, beaming ear to ear.

"Do you think your fans realize I'm your wife when they spot you out in public?" I ask as we go back to filling our plates with food.

"Who knows," Jace says with a shrug. "I think some of them prefer to pretend you don't exist."

He gives me an evil smile and I laugh. "You're probably right."

We sit down at the large table and another woman walks up to Jace, wanting a photo. And then another.

I take a bite of the fluffiest pancake I've ever had in my life. It's annoying that we're being constantly interrupted by Jace's fans, but at least the food is good. I'd forgotten to get bacon for myself while I was taking that first photo, so I reach over and steal a piece from Jace's plate while he's talking to a fan.

The next thing I know, there's a line of women waiting to talk to him. We're at the breakfast table for crying out loud. People can be so rude. Just across the table, a camera is focused on me. I take a sip of orange juice and then stand up. My heavy wooden chair scrapes loudly across the floor.

"Excuse me!" I call out to the room in general. Not many people notice so I call out even louder. "Hello! Everyone, can I have your attention please?" In the corner of my eye, I notice the cameraman moving closer, probably zooming in on my face. I ignore it and hold out my hand toward Jace.

"Yes, this is the famous motocross racer, Jace Adams. If you'd like a photo with him, please give him just a few minutes to finish his freaking breakfast. Then I'll meet you in the hallway and take as many pictures of you and him as you want. Just please, let us eat first!"

The first person in the line that had been formed by Jace looks mortified. "Sorry," she says before turning away.

Jace puts an arm around me and kisses my cheek. "Great idea, babe."

Slowly, everyone leaves us alone so we can sit and finish our meal. The camera guy walks away. I get the weird feeling he's disappointed.

I GUESS MY LITTLE PLAN BACKFIRED. I WAS MOSTLY BEING sarcastic when I'd stood up and offered to take pictures for people after we've finished eating. I figured my little stunt would make everyone realize how rude they were being, and then they'd leave us alone.

Nope.

We were able to finish our breakfast, at least. But then as soon as we stood up, a crowd of mostly women followed us into the hallway. They all took turns taking pictures with my husband while I waited patiently, helping a few of them take the photos. But now it's finally over, and I think Jace had to personally meet every woman in this lodge in the process.

With the cameras following us, Jace and I take a little walk around the lodge. Every inch of the place is decorated and they must have cinnamon, fir tree, and vanilla scents piped in from some hidden vents because every room smells delightful. It somehow manages to feel like a luxurious vacation as well as a nostalgic trip down memory lane because all of this holiday cheer reminds me of being a kid. I've always loved Christmas, and now that I have a kid of my own, I love it even more.

I text Becca to check in while we walk around the lodge. I tell her I'll try to call her later when I'm in the bathroom because I don't want the cameras to film a private conversation with my kid. He's a kid, and I don't want him blasted all over TV without him being old enough to consent to it.

Becca assures me that Jett is doing great and that they're having a ton of fun. He's probably completely spoiled rotten by now.

When I'm finished texting, I put my phone into my pajama pants pockets, which is uncomfortable because the pants are too light and the phone is too heavy. I reach out and hold Jace's hand as we step into the hotel gift shop. All of the stuff in here is exactly like the things in town—Christmas over-load. I wander over to a community bulletin board and read the flyers, looking for something fun to do.

"There's a class on rock painting?" Jace says, pointing at a small yellow flier. "I wonder what people paint on rocks."

"Oooh, glass blowing!" I say, pointing at another flier, only to realize that the dates are old and the glass blowing classes were last week. Bummer.

An older man walks up to us, hands in his pockets while he looks over the bulletin board.

"Are you two looking for something to do?" he asks.

He's wearing regular blue jeans and a brown sweater. Even his shoes are just plain sneakers. This might be the first person I've seen in Cheer who isn't dressed like a billboard for Christmas decorations.

"Yes, we are," I say. "Do you have any suggestions?"

He smiles. "Well, we can always use more wrappers."

"Rappers?" Jace says, quirking an eyebrow. "I don't exactly have that talent."

The man chuckles. "I mean wrapping paper wrappers. I volunteer down at the church. You may have seen it when you arrived. It's that little white building way at the end of the road."

I nod, because I do remember it. It's old school, with a little steeple and everything. He also tells us his name is Marcus, and says he's lived here in Cheer with his wife for ten years. They moved here from Oklahoma. He continues, "We collect toys and gifts all year long and then we wrap them up and donate to families in need. We have hundreds of presents to wrap this month, so we're happy to have some help if you're up for it."

I look over at Jace, giving him my best puppy eyes smile in the hopes that I'll convince him to say yes. "Can we do it?"

He's already giving me basically the same look and my heart warms because I know he's thinking the same thing I am. "That sounds fun."

Marcus offers to drive us there in fifteen minutes, giving us time to go back up to our room and change into better clothes. Jace and I rush up to the third floor and put on one of our hilariously spirited new outfits. Then we're back downstairs and out in the parking lot, leaving the camera guys struggling to catch up after we get in Marcus's small Honda.

"Sorry about the cameras," Jace says. We both look out the windows, watching as the camera crew scrambles to get into their van to follow us. It's kind of hilarious watching them try to keep up.

"It's all good," Marcus says, waving his hand. "We're used to the cameras by now."

"Do a lot of reality TV shows film here?" I ask.

He nods. "Oh, yes. Cheer is a popular destination for tourists and Hollywood. No one even blinks an eye anymore when they see cameras following people around. We're used to it. I don't really like it much, but I'm used to it. Of course, no one has ever offered to help me wrap presents before, so you two are very fine people."

I don't realize I'm grinning from ear to ear until I catch a glimpse of myself in the rearview mirror. This is really fun. I love wrapping presents and I love helping out the community. Also, a big part of me is just excited to be in a car ride without the cameras watching me. Then, like a punch to the gut, I get a weird feeling. What if Marcus is a plant? What if this car is filled with hidden cameras?

Jace must get the same idea I do, because I notice him looking around the car. I don't see anything out of the ordinary though, and within a couple of minutes, Marcus pulls up to the cute little church. There's a big metal barn in the back of the property and that's where the presents are. I know he said he had hundreds of gifts to wrap, but whoa. There are literally hundreds—probably thousands—of toys, clothes, household items, and other gifts, all laid out on tables and piled on the floor. Then there are five tables filled with boxes of wrapping paper, tape, and ribbons. Two middle-aged women stand at two tables, wrapping presents.

"I brought some help!" Marcus says, introducing us to the small group.

"This is my wife, Jannelle," he says, sliding an arm around the woman at the first table. "And this is my sister, Mary-Ellen."

The women welcome us and thank us for helping. They explain how each gift has a tag on it already, so we just wrap it up, then tape the name tag so they know where it goes. Jace is surprisingly good at the task, and we have a lot of fun with Marcus and the ladies. We learn that Marcus and Jannelle have been married for thirty-five years.

"Do you have any marriage advice for us?" Jace asks as he reaches across the table for some blue ribbon.

"Never go to bed angry," Marcus says.

"Yeah, stay up late so you can plot revenge,"

Jannelle says. She bursts into laughter and Marcus joins her.

"Always have a sense of humor, too," he says, smiling at his wife. "Laughter gets us through everything."

"I think when you're soulmates, it just works." Jannelle looks over at her husband. "It's easy. Everything just works."

"Aww." I can't believe I'm a little teary-eyed right now, but watching a couple be so in love after thirty-five years is really moving. That's longer than I've been alive. I look over at Jace.

"I love you," I say.

He leans forward and smacks a kiss on my lips. "I love you too, Bay."

It's a perfect, special moment. And it's ruined a few seconds later when the two camera guys come bursting into the room, having finally caught up with us. The ladies don't seem to mind, which is good. I like it here and I'd hate to get kicked out because of a stupid TV show.

We spend hours wrapping presents and listening to our new friends talk about marriage and the town of Cheer, and all the great charitable work they do each year. Mary-Ellen insists on feeding us lunch and serving us tea and cookies a couple hours later. Jace and I wrap a ton of presents, and before I know it, it's starting to get dark outside.

Marcus drives us back to the lodge. A cold front has just blown in and the chill in the air makes it really feel like Christmas. The main stretch of Cheer is even more beautiful at night when the lights are glowing and twinkling everywhere you look, but I'm feeling pretty tired and it's getting colder by the minute, so I don't want to walk around tonight.

"I kind of just want to watch a movie," I tell Jace as we're walking back inside the lodge. "Is that cool with you?"

We step into the elevator and the camera guy follows us, making the space feel extra cramped.

Jace holds my hand. "Sounds good to me. Do you have a movie in mind?"

"Elf?"

He grins. "Perfect."

This time, it's not as horrifying when we crawl into bed and there's a guy on the couch filming us the whole time. Still horrifying, just… not as much. We put the movie on the massive TV and cuddle up in the soft blankets and fluffy pillows. I keep glancing at the clock, waiting for midnight so the camera guy will leave and we'll get a tiny spec of privacy.

But it's hard to stay awake when I'm wrapped up cozy, snuggled up to Jace, and before I know it, I fall asleep.

THE NEXT MORNING, WE'RE NOT RUDELY WOKEN UP BY THE cameraman. We're already awake when he arrives, much to his surprise. The coolest, most magical thing happened overnight. Jace woke me up at four this morning. He was so excited as he gently woke me up, I almost thought he was Jett for a minute.

"It's snowing," he whispered.

I bolted out of bed.

We've only seen snow a few times in our lives. It doesn't happen much in Texas, especially not the southern part where we live. But Cheer is a couple hundred miles north of our hometown, and it gets a little colder here. The cold front brought snow with it, and Jace and I had slipped out onto the balcony at four in the morning and watched the beautiful white tufts fall to the ground. It was the best part of this vacation so far. Just the love of my life, and me, under a starry night sky, feeling snowflakes on our hair and landing on our fingertips.

When the doorbell rings this time, I cheerfully walk over and let the cameraman inside. The red blinking light is on, and I know the rules say I'm not allowed to talk to him, but it feels really weird not knowing his name. Angel had briefly told us that first day, but I don't remember it because I was too nervous to pay attention. I can't just keep calling him "the cameraman" because it feels rude.

"Hey, what's your name?" I ask the big shiny camera lens that's in my face.

He pokes his head out from behind the camera. "Jack."

"Cool. Nice to meet you, Jack."

He nods once, probably terrified to get in trouble, then he moves his face back behind the camera.

Maybe it's because I'm so excited for the snow, or maybe it's that fifty thousand dollars we're getting paid, but I'm in a good mood today and I want him to get some good footage. So I put on a friendly face and try to act like someone who would be on a reality TV show.

"Oh my gosh, look outside!" I gasp, running to

the large glass doors that open onto our balcony. "It's snowing!"

Jack follows closely, filming my every move.

"Babe!" I call out to Jace, who is in the kitchenette area, pouring two cups of coffee. "It's snowing!"

He picks up on what I'm doing, and he joins me, handing me a cup of coffee. "Wow, it's beautiful."

We step out onto the balcony and basically reenact what we did early this morning when we were alone. I stand against the balcony railing, sipping my coffee while Jace wraps an arm around me.

"It's almost as beautiful as you," he whispers, kissing my cheek.

The camera is just inches away from us, so I know it caught every word. The TV producers will love this crap. After all, it's no secret in the motocross community that Jace is married to the love of his life. Me. We're giving them excellent footage right now. It makes my heart beat a little quicker knowing that these scenes will totally be chosen for the episode. I hope my hair looks okay.

The phone rings at the same time again this morning, and we are once again invited to breakfast with Mrs. Claus. I chose one of my Christmas outfits

—a candy cane sweater dress and the black sandals I wore on my trip here. Jace wears khaki board shorts that have little Santa beard graphics all over them and a red T-shirt that says ho ho ho. It's tacky and dorky but we're embracing it.

When we get down to the breakfast hall, Mrs. Claus gives us a confused look. "Honey, you're going to freeze to death in that outfit."

"Oh, I feel fine," Jace says.

She peers at us as if we've grown another head. "It's much, much too cold out for clothes like this. I hope you two have good warm clothes in your suitcases?"

"We don't have suitcases," I say with a chuckle.

A grown man who is dressed like an elf—with the big fake ears and everything—approaches us. "Don't worry, Mrs. Claus, they won't be venturing outside any time soon," he says. "The town is shut down."

"What?" I blurt out. "Why?"

"It's too cold. Ice all over the roads. They've declared a Stay at Home order."

"Oh, well goodness, that is good luck then," Mrs. Claus says, patting me on the arm. "You two will be nice and warm here in the lodge."

Breakfast is a lot like yesterday, minus a million

fans trying to talk to Jace. Now it's like no one cares that he's here at all. Only a handful of people even eat breakfast this morning, and they're all talking about the freak snowstorm we had last night. Apparently a few inches of snow in any other state that's used to snow isn't a big deal. But here in Texas where it rarely snows, our roads and cars aren't built for it so everything just shuts down. All the shops on Main Street are closed today. There's nothing to do but hang out around the lodge.

After we eat breakfast, Jace and I walk back up to our room with Jack following behind us. I've noticed that when we're here in the lodge, we typically have just him following us, but when we go out places, the other guy joins him so they can film us from two different angles. I know the camera guys are staying in the lodge too, because I asked Angel when we talked with her yesterday. Speaking of...

"I wonder if Angel is staying here at the lodge?" I ask Jace as we step onto the elevator.

"She probably is, just because it's easier to be close to us," he says. "She loves popping in unexpectedly."

I nod. "I was thinking that, too. And if we're stuck inside all day that means she'll probably come bother us."

He playfully smacks my butt. "We should just snuggle in bed all day and make her feel uncomfortable when she does come around."

I give him a sultry smile, which is lost on our future television audience because the camera is facing my back. "I like the way you think, Mr. Adams."

In our room, we play one of the endless Christmas movies on the television and raid the mini bar. There's several packets of hot chocolate, so Jace makes us each a cup and then we find board games in a closet. I spread out the games on the bed and we play them for hours, just hanging out and enjoying the quiet time together, even if Jack is sitting on the couch filming us.

I keep expecting Angel to pop in and annoy us, but no one comes by, not even Mrs. Claus to make sure we're wearing warm enough clothes. We order room service for lunch, and then we sneak into the bathroom to video chat with Jett.

He's wearing a jacket I've never seen before. Becca explains that they went to Old Navy and she got him some stuff because she can't help herself. He's still having a blast being with his honorary aunt and uncle and he doesn't care that we'll be gone one more night before we come home. In fact, we could probably be gone for months and he would be happy with how spoiled he is over at the Park residence.

We get room service again for dinner, and Jace wants to snuggle under the covers after we eat, but I feel so awkward with Jack in the room. Having a camera on me all the time is starting to wear on me, even though the payout in the end will totally be worth it.

Around nightfall, our cheery doorbell goes off.

"There she is," Jace says, stretching his arms out as he sits up in bed. We've been watching Christmas movies and playing board games all day. I'm kind of surprised it's dark already.

He walks over to answer the door, but it's not Angel. It's the guy who was dressed like an elf this morning. He's *still* dressed like an elf.

"I'm pleased to let you know the snow has melted from the roads, making them safe again. And since you are our honored guests, we have arranged a romantic horse-drawn carriage ride for you this evening."

Jace looks back at me with a surprised look on his face. "That sounds fun. What do you think?"

"I love it!" I jump out of bed.

The human elf tells us to meet downstairs by the

front doors. He also reminds us to dress warm. We throw on all the warm Christmas-themed clothes we have and head downstairs. Right in the front, at the valet drop off, waits a beautiful shiny red carriage with a gorgeous black Clysdale standing regally at the ready. The driver says he'll be back in just a moment.

Jace and I climb inside, sitting on the plush leather seat. It's taller than I thought it would be, and it kind of reminds me of what Santa's sleigh looks like in the movies, except instead of nine reindeer, this carriage is pulled by one massive horse.

"We gotta show Jett," Jace says, pulling out his phone. We video chat with him again and Jace shows him the carriage and the horse. Jett thinks it's pretty cool, but then he says he needs to get back to playing video games with Park.

"That kid…" I say with a chuckle.

We're still waiting on the driver to come back, so Jace starts playing the I-Spy game that we play with Jett when we're on long car rides. We play for a while, laughing and enjoying each other's company.

When the driver returns, he looks flustered. "So sorry about the wait," he says, climbing up into the driver's seat at the front of the carriage. "I was afraid you would have left by now."

"What do you mean?" Jace says.

The driver shuffles in his seat. "Well, it's been over an hour, sir. I'm really sorry for the wait."

"It's been an hour?" I say, looking at the time on my phone. "Wow, it only feels like maybe ten minutes."

The driver's eyebrows press together in the middle. "You're sitting out here in the cold for over an hour and didn't even realize it?"

I shrug. "Guess not. I was having too much fun just hanging out with Jace."

My husband smiles. "Same here."

Chapter Eleven

This is our third and final day in Cheer, Texas, which is also our last day being filmed. While the lodge is beautiful and the Christmasy town has been fun, entertaining, and a bit hilarious, I find myself longing for home. I miss having my rambunctious but adorable son around me all the time. After breakfast, I slip into the bathroom and run the shower so Jack keeps his camera off me, and then I video chat with Jett for a little while. I tell him I miss him and I can't wait to come home.

When I emerge from the bathroom, Jack gives me a questioning look from behind his camera. He's probably confused about why I exited the bathroom wearing the same clothes I had on this morning, with dry hair and absolutely zero evidence that I just showered. I grin at him, not feeling bad at all for the teensy lie.

Jace has decided to raid the mini-fridge and has set up a few sodas on the counter.

"What are you doing?"

"Trying to decide if a Sprite mixed with Dr. Pepper would taste good."

"Um, why?" I say with a little laugh.

He shrugs. "We're on vacation, baby. Why not live on the wild side?"

"We're about to go on an awesome adventure, you dork." I reach over and pour one can of soda into a glass, then crack open the other, emptying it into the cup. I hold it up to him. "This is your big moment. Live on the wild side, babe."

He takes a sip, holds it in his mouth for a second, pursing his lips in thought. Then he swallows.

"Well?" I ask.

"It's not terrible, but it needs ice."

Our ice bucket is now filled with water from last night's melted ice. I grab the bucket. "I'll go get some more for your dorky experiment."

He takes another sip of his soda concoction and snaps his fingers, pointing at me. "You're the best, babe."

Out in the hallway, I suddenly feel weird. I turn

around, looking down the long, empty hallway. Then I turn back to look at our suite door. Then it hits me: Jack didn't follow me out here.

I am alone.

Truly alone. No camera recording my every move.

I walk with a pep in my step down toward the little room with an ice maker and vending machines. A sign on the machine tells me it's out of service. No worries—I'll just go to another floor and use that machine and if it takes me longer, that's just more time without a camera recording me.

I step into the elevator. The doors start to close, and then a hand reaches in and stops it.

"Wait for me!" a guy says as he rushes inside.

But he's not just any guy. He's tanned, muscled, with sopping wet blonde hair. And he's shirtless, wearing just black board shorts, flip flops, and carrying a towel in his hand. He offers me a smoldering smile that's so damn smoldering, it has to be something he practices daily in the mirror.

What a tool.

"Hey, how are ya?" he says, leaning against the back wall of the elevator as the doors slowly close. He throws the towel around the back of his neck and holds onto each end in his hands.

"I'm fine," I reply, pressing the button for the second floor while holding the ice bucket in my other hand. "What floor do you want?"

"Whatever floor you're going to."

I look at him, confused. He smirks.

Oh god, is he flirting with me?

"If you're trying to flirt with me, you should know that I'm married," I say flatly.

His lips quirk up in a smirky grin that makes the hairs on the back of my neck stand up. At least I have this metal ice bucket to smash against his face if he tries anything. And the elevator ride will be over soon, luckily. This guy is giving me the creeps.

"I'm not trying to flirt with you," he says, flexing his arms while he holds onto the towel so that his biceps bulge. "I *am* flirting with you."

I hold up my left hand, showing off the gorgeous, custom made diamond ring Jace gave to me years ago. "Dude, I'm married."

"I don't care." His smile widens. "I've never seen a woman as beautiful as you are. I can feel a connection between us, can't you?"

My brows pull together as I wonder if I'm really hearing what I think I'm hearing. "Are you drunk or high or something?" I ask with a snort. "What kind of guy just hits on a random married woman who is wearing Christmas pajamas?"

"It might sound crazy, but I know what I want in a woman and you're clearly the whole package. I don't even care about that man of yours. I bet I make more money than him. I can give you a better life than he can, I promise you that."

I burst out laughing, then I turn back toward the elevator doors, waiting for them to open. It's been way longer than it should take for an elevator just to travel from the third floor to the second. This guy's flirting might actually work on other women, but I'm married to Jace Adams. It doesn't get any better than that.

The elevator clunks to a stop. I wait a moment, but the doors don't open.

"That's weird," the guy says.

He moves away from the back wall and walks up to the doors. We stare at them for several seconds, and nothing happens. He reaches over and presses the door open button, but it doesn't do anything. My heart starts beating a little quicker.

"What the hell is happening?" I say. I'm not really talking to the shirtless guy next to me. I just have this panicked need to speak out loud.

"It's okay, we'll just call for help." He pushes the

emergency alert button on the elevator. It lights up. A few seconds later, a voice speaks through the little speaker in the wall.

"Cheer City Emergency Services."

"Uh, hi. I'm stuck in an elevator," he says. He looks at me and whispers, "with a beautiful woman."

I roll my eyes.

The speaker crackles. "Okay, please remain calm. Which building are you in?"

"The Cheer Lodge*."

"Okay, I see there's a problem with the main circuit board. We'll head over to fix it. It should take about an hour."

"An hour?" I screech. "Are you serious?"

"Yes, ma'am," the voice says. "May I ask how many people are in there right now?"

"There's two of us," I say.

"Does anyone have any pressing emergency health conditions?"

"Well, no," I say.

"We'll do our best, but expect an hour wait."

The call ends and I slump against the wall. "I can't believe I'm stuck in an elevator for a freaking hour," I mutter. I don't even have my phone on me to call Jace. He's going to be so worried, but hopefully a staff member will alert him to what happened.

"I consider it a blessing." The shirtless guy makes another smoldering look my way. "My name is Tyson, by the way. What's yours?"

"You can call me *Mrs.* Adams," I say, emphasizing the pronunciation of Mrs.

"I can respect your decision to act like you're not enticed by my offer," Tyson says. "I mean, you're probably visiting this lodge with your husband, right?"

"Of course. Because we're happily married and we take vacations together."

He chuckles. "Then why did he make you go get ice all by yourself?"

Okay now I'm a bit offended. "Because he's not a sexist pig who thinks women need to be controlled," I say. "My husband respects me, and I respect him."

Tyson drags in a long, deep breath. He leans back against the hand railing that lines three walls of the elevator. "Fine. I guess I'll leave you alone. It's just sad, seeing such a beautiful woman and knowing you could be my soulmate." He exhales, frowning a bit. It still seems like he's trying really hard to be sexy with everything he does. That's just it—he tries too hard.

He frowns. "I hate thinking I could have met the love of my life today and then I just let her go." He holds out his hands, gesturing to the elevator. "I mean... we got stuck in an elevator together. That kind of feels like fate, don't you think?"

"Dude, let me give you some advice, okay?" I take a deep breath, trying to focus on anything else besides the fact that I'm *stuck in a freaking elevator*. "You're obviously an attractive guy. You shouldn't have any problems finding a girlfriend, except I bet you do have problems because you act like this. Do you really think it's attractive to tell me to leave my husband within five seconds of meeting me? Am I supposed to have faith in you being a good person when you act like that? Do you really think that I could leave my husband, marry you, and then live my life not being worried that you'll just leave me for the next woman you lay eyes on?"

He stares at me, stunned. His mouth opens and closes, like he wants to talk but can't quite figure out what to say.

"That's what you're doing wrong," I say. "If you see a woman and you'd like to ask her out, ask her out. If she says no, then accept that answer and move on. Because I guarantee you that trying to steal a woman away from her husband like you did to me isn't going to get you a happily ever after."

Tyson's tanned cheeks actually flush red. He stands there looking awkward and sheepish for a few seconds. "I'm sorry," he mutters.

And that's when it hits me. I can't believe—after these last few days—that I didn't see it coming from a mile away. Tyson is a paid actor. He knew exactly what to say until I flipped the script on him and now he's bashful and awkward because he didn't prepare for me to react this way.

I tip my head back and stare at the roof of the elevator as a laugh pours out of me. "Oh my gosh," I say slowly, shaking my head. "I'm so dumb. This was obviously a set up."

I laugh so hard I snort. "Where's the camera?" I say, looking around. "It's hidden in here somewhere, isn't it?" I press my face up to the speaker near the emergency button. Then I look in the corners and up high at the roof. I don't see anything, but I know it's there. That's why Jack didn't bother following me outside with his camera. This whole thing was already set up.

Tyson doesn't admit it, but he also doesn't deny it, which is all the proof I need. I take a deep breath, able to relax a bit more because at least now I know this guy isn't some kind of crazy murderer. He's probably some male model trying to break into acting.

I push the emergency button again. When the speaker crackles to life, I speak before whoever is on the other end has a chance to.

"The gig is up, guys. I'm not falling for this obvious Reality TV scam. Can you please let me out of here now? I have to pee."

The elevator doors open and Jack is standing just outside of them, camera on his shoulder. I walk right up to the round lens and roll my eyes. "Nice try."

AND JUST LIKE THAT, THIS WEIRD ADVENTURE IS COMING to an end. The limo Hummer arrives, pulling up into the valet drop-off section of the lodge. Mrs. Claus packed us breakfast to-go, and Angel is standing near the limo when we walk outside. There's still a chill in the air, and in fact, it's even colder than usual. We carry our new clothes in large gift bags from the lodge's gift shop.

The first thing I notice when we step outside is the lack of cameras. It's just Angel, standing there in a sleek black pants suit, her arms crossed over her chest. Her gaze seems far away, as if her thoughts are on something else right now.

"Your luggage is in the back," she says, making a

sweeping gesture toward the limo as if daring us to go verify it for ourselves.

"Sounds good," Jace says politely.

The limo driver is the same guy from before, and he steps out and opens the car door for us. "So very sorry about the luggage mishap," the man says apologetically.

"Oh, it's fine," I say. "We got some cute new clothes that'll make sure we never forget this trip."

Angel snorts out a laugh. It's the most serious-sounding laugh ever.

"What's wrong?" I ask her.

"Oh, well I guess I can't be mad at you two," she says, which startles me. "You can't help it."

"Wait, why would you be mad at us?" I ask. "What did we do wrong?"

She points to her fingers, listing things off. "You didn't care one bit that your luggage was gone. You somehow magically had hundreds of dollars of cash to pay for clothes when your card didn't work, the screaming fangirls didn't bother you—in fact you offered to help them take a photo with your man!" she says, rolling her eyes in wonderment at that last part.

She sighs. "The fake icy road shut down didn't

faze you. You didn't mind waiting an hour and a half in a cold horse carriage. In fact, you made a fun game out of it! The boring Christmas-only TV channels only made you cuddle up and enjoy each other's company. Early wakeup calls didn't bother you. You didn't even flirt for one teensy second with the hottest male model I've ever hired." She throws her hands up as a delirious little laugh escapes her. "You two are impossible. You love each other too much!"

"What's wrong with loving each other?" I ask.

"Well, nothing in real life," she says. "But it makes for real shit Reality TV."

Jace chuckles, putting an arm around me. "I'm sorry, Angel. We tried our best."

She waves a dismissive hand toward us. "No worries. My boss will just have to get over it. A deal is a deal, and you'll still earn the money if we can't air your episode."

"Wait, you're not going to air it?" I ask, suddenly a little disappointed even though I hated every second of being filmed all weekend.

She shakes her head. "Nope. None of the footage was dramatic enough. It would make for boring TV."

Jace and I exchange a look. I shrug. "At least we get our pool!"

He nods. "Yep. Best free vacation ever."

Chapter Thirteen

Jett

Present Day

"And, that's that," Dad says, smiling at Mom. "We got a free vacation and bought a pool with our earnings."

"I wish someone would offer us a bunch of money to film another TV show," Mom says playfully. "I could use a new car."

"I can't believe I never knew this," I say, mouth open in shock. "I mean... I think I remember staying with Park and Becca for a few days when I was little. But I guess I never knew what you were doing."

Mom sips her hot chocolate. "We thought it

would be fun to surprise you with watching the TV show when it aired, but then it never did, so we just kind of forgot about it."

Brooke runs up to our parents holding a big box wrapped in pink Christmas wrapping paper. "Can I open this?"

"Yes you may," Mom says. Her eyes sparkle when she talks to my little sister.

Sometimes I think it's a little weird that my parents have such a young child when I'm already grown and married, but they were young parents when they had me, and having Brooke seems to make them really happy. I'm glad they're happy, and my sister is pretty cool. I think being her big brother has given me experience to help be a good dad myself.

My parents' attention goes to the kids as they rip open presents and shriek in excitement at each one. Park and Becca spoil their young son just as much as my parents spoil my sister. I realize now as I sit here, arm wrapped around Keanna, that I have an amazing family. I am so unbelievably lucky.

Keanna lifts her head up to look at me while she leans against my chest. "How romantic was that story?" she muses. "Your parents love each other so much that no drama can come between them."

"That's them alright," I say, glancing over at my parents. Dad is currently wearing a princess tiara that Brooke put on top of his head and Mom is ripping open a back of AA batteries to put in Brooke's new toy.

"There's only one thing more romantic than their love," Keanna says so softly that only I can hear.

I reach out and rest my hand on her pregnant stomach. "And what's that?" I ask.

She grins. "Our love."

The end

Want to be the first to know about new books, exclusive giveaways, and more?

Join Amy Sparling's newsletter! You'll know when her new books release and get exclusive book and gift card giveaways. You can unsubscribe at any time. I give away a $10 gift card to a random subscriber with each newsletter!

Sign up here: http://eepurl.com/bTmkPX

About the Author

Amy Sparling is the bestselling author of books for teens and the teens at heart. She lives on the coast of Texas with her family, her spoiled rotten pets, and a huge pile of books. She graduated with a degree in English and has worked at a bookstore, coffee shop, and a fashion boutique. Her fashion skills aren't the best, but luckily she turned her love of coffee and books into a writing career that means she can work in her pajamas. Her favorite things are coffee, book boyfriends, and Netflix binges.

She's always loved reading books from R. L. Stine's Fear Street series, to The Baby Sitter's Club series by Ann, Martin, and of course, Twilight. She started writing her own books in 2010 and now publishes several books a year. Connect with her on one of the links below.

www.AmySparling.com

facebook.com/authoramysparling

bookbub.com/profile/amy-sparling

goodreads.com/Amy_Sparling

instagram.com/writeamysparling

www.ingramcontent.com/pod-product-compliance
Lightning Source LLC
Chambersburg PA
CBHW031335160726
47993CB00002B/691